One Kiss, One Hug!

Jason Chapman

RED FOX

'. . .and they all lived *happily ever after,*' whispered Daddy Bear.

He kissed and hugged Ben and Ursula goodnight.
Ursula went to sleep straight away.

'Night night, snuggle down,' said Daddy Bear
and he went downstairs.
But Ben didn't snuggle down.

He couldn't get to sleep at all. He turned this way and he turned that way. He even tried closing his eyes and counting salmon, but that only made him hungry.

A short while later, Mummy and
Daddy Bear were just about to have
supper when they heard Ben calling,
'Mummy, you haven't come to say goodnight.'
Mummy Bear put down her plate
and raced upstairs.

'Can I have one kiss and one hug?'
asked Ben.

Mummy Bear gave him a kiss and a hug,
tucked him into bed and went downstairs.

After supper, Mummy and Daddy Bear were washing the dishes when they heard Ben call, 'I can't sleep!'

Mummy Bear sighed. 'Your turn,' she said,
and Daddy Bear marched up the stairs.

'Shhh,' said Daddy Bear.
'But I can't sleep,' said Ben. 'Can I have
one more kiss and one more hug?'
'Just one more kiss and one more hug and then you
really must try to get to sleep,' said Daddy Bear.

He gave Ben a kiss and a hug
and went back downstairs.

'Ice cream?' asked Mummy Bear.
'Now that is a good idea,' said Daddy Bear.

Mummy and Daddy Bear snuggled together in front of the fire.
'Mmm, honey and vanilla ice cream. My favourite!'
said Mummy Bear.

Meanwhile, Ben still couldn't get to sleep.

He flipped his pillow over to
see if it was more comfortable
and flipped it back.

He pushed the cover off
when he felt hot and pulled it
on again when he got cold.

Nothing was working.
There was only one thing
left to do. . .

'Oh no, this is too much!' said Mummy Bear.
Up the stairs she went while Daddy Bear helped himself
to more than his share of the ice cream.

'Just **one** more kiss and **one** more hug,' said Ben.
'Now, Ben, that's enough. It's time you were asleep.'

Mummy Bear gave him a kiss and a hug
and went back downstairs.

All had been quiet for some time now so Daddy Bear
sat down and opened up his book. Just at that moment,
bellowing down the stairs, Ben shouted,

'one kiss,
one hug!'

'I don't believe it!' said Daddy Bear.
He dropped his book and stomped upstairs grumbling.
'He'll wake his sister up with all this noise.'

But Daddy's stomping disturbed Ursula.

'Shhh, Daddy!' said Ben. 'You'll wake up Ursula.'

Daddy Bear's eyes bulged and his chest puffed out a little.

'One kiss, one hug?' whispered Ben.
'The last one!' said Daddy Bear very slowly
and very quietly, and then he went back downstairs.

Ben pulled the blanket up over his head
and closed his eyes tightly,
determined to get to sleep.

Ursula stirred a little more and then woke up.
She looked for Ben but couldn't see him
next to her and she started to cry.

Mummy and Daddy Bear looked
at each other in disbelief.
Now Ursula was awake too!

The two very weary and worn-out bears
trudged up the stairs.

But by the time they reached the little bears' room,
both Ursula and Ben were fast asleep.
Ben had snuggled up to his little sister and given her. . .

one kiss and one hug.

For George,
Iris & Oriel
with love,
Daddy x

ONE   KISS,   ONE   HUG
A RED FOX BOOK   978 1 782 95579 5
First   published   in   Great   Britain   by   Red   Fox,
an   imprint   of   Random House   Children's   Books
A Random House Group Company   This edition published 2012
10 9 8 7 6 5 4 3 2 1   Copyright © Jason Chapman, 2012
The right of Jason Chapman to be identified as the author of this work has been
asserted in accordance with the Copyright, Designs and Patents Act 1988.
All   rights   reserved.   No   part   of   this   publication   may   be
reproduced, stored in a retrieval system, or transmitted in any form
or   by   any   means,   electronic,   mechanical,   photocopying,
recording or otherwise, without the prior permission of the publishers.
Red Fox Books are published by Random House Children's Books,
61–63   Uxbridge   Road,   London   W5   5SA
www.**kidsatrandomhouse**.co.uk   www.**randomhouse**.co.uk
Addresses   for   companies   within   The   Random   House
Group   Limited   can   be   found   at:
w w w . r a n d o m h o u s e . c o . u k / o f f i c e s . h t m
THE   RANDOM   HOUSE   GROUP
Limited   Reg.   No.   954009
A   CIP   catalogue   record   for   this
book   is   available   from   the
British   Library.
Printed   in
China